Crazy Creatures

by

Gill Arbuthnott

Illustrated by Shona Grant

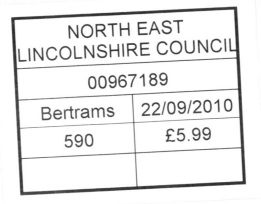
You do not need to read this page –
just get on with the book!

First published in 2007 in Great Britain by
Barrington Stoke Ltd
18 Walker Street, Edinburgh, EH3 7LP

www.barringtonstoke.co.uk

Reprinted 2008, 2009

ISBN: 978-1-84299-457-3

Printed in Great Britain by Bell & Bain Ltd

For Graham 'Prof' Ferguson,
in memory of unsuccessful rabbit
hunting on the Isle of May ...

Intro

If you tried to invent an animal that did something really odd, I think you'd find it already existed. In fact, that it had existed for millions of years. That's one of the things I love about animals. They don't have to have cute little furry faces to appeal to me. In fact, they don't need to have faces at all.

I'd like to show you some of the crazy creatures I really like. I've put them into four sections: **Yuk!, Weapons, Weird and Wonderful,** and **Lazy Bones**. This means you can make up your own mind which ones you don't want to read when you're eating your breakfast! At the end of the book there are also some **Fantastic Facts** that you can use to impress your friends – wouldn't you like to know which animal to use to commit the perfect murder?

Contents

Chapter 1
Yuk!

Vampire Bats

Yes! Vampires really do exist! Vampire bats live in South America, and yes, they do suck blood. They fly or creep silently onto a sleeping animal. Their front teeth are razor sharp. They use them to bite the animal very gently, so they don't wake it up. They often bite large mammals like cows or humans. When they bite they put their spit (saliva) into the wound, and this

stops the blood from clotting. The bats
don't really suck the blood, they just lick it
up as the wound bleeds. They need about
two big spoons of blood a day.

They don't often attack dogs. Some
people think this is because dogs can hear
the high squeaks that bats use to find their

way around, so the bats can't creep up on them.

A drug has been made based on bat spit to stop blood clotting in humans. It's called – wait for it – *draculin*!

Fulmars

Fulmars are birds that look a lot like seagulls with very stiff wings. They don't hang around in towns like seagulls, unless the towns are near the sea. They nest on cliffs, and that keeps them and their chicks safe most of the time, but if they think you are going to hurt them they don't fly away or try to peck you. Oh no, it's much smellier than that. They're sick all over you. Lovely! They eat fish, including scraps thrown off fishing boats. They also love dead seal, most of all if it's been floating around for a while. When they've eaten it, the stuff gets *very* smelly.

Don't wear your best clothes if you want
to annoy a fulmar, because the smell won't
come out – ever. All you can do is burn
your clothes. And stand well away from the
fire when you do it.

Sea Cucumbers

You thought fulmars were bad, but it gets even more disgusting!

You can see what sea cucumbers look like on the front cover of the book. They must be one of the most boring animals in the sea. They come from the same family as starfish. They look as if they've put all five arms together above their heads and fallen over onto their side. They creep around very slowly, eating tiny bits and pieces. If another animal attacks one and tries to eat it, the sea cucumber isn't just sick on it but vomits up its guts all over its enemy. The guts are very sticky, and while the other animal is busy trying to scrape the stuff off itself, the sea cucumber gets away – very slowly! If it does get away, it grows a new set of guts, and in about two weeks, it's ready to puke again.

You find sea cucumbers in shallow water anywhere the sea is warm (that rules Britain out). Children in countries that have them often use them as water pistols. They squeeze them until they spray their guts all over someone. I don't suppose it's a very popular game with the person who has to wash their clothes ...

Hag Fish

Not a very pretty name, it's true. But they really don't deserve a nice name. These dear little fish are about as slimy as it's possible to be. They look like water snakes or eels and have no bones – they don't even have a jaw. They don't have a proper mouth but their face has a sort of sucker on the front, covered with hooks, and with a spiny tongue in the middle. They use this to attach themselves to a fish and stay stuck to it. Then they use their tongue to scrape away at its flesh. The poor fish gets eaten alive!

Maggots

Maggots are our friends. You didn't expect that, did you? But it's true. If it wasn't for maggots we'd be knee deep in dead animals. Maggots help get rid of all the bodies. But what are maggots? Cute little baby blue-bottle flies! (Well, maybe they look cute to their mums.) And what do they like to eat? Meat – lots of it – but it has to be rotting. Yummy.

When an animal dies, a blue-bottle will find it within an hour and lay a few hundred eggs on it. When the maggots hatch out of the eggs they start eating, and don't stop until they've finished every scrap. Once they've eaten all they can, they change into blue-bottles.

So, could you be eaten alive by maggots? Well, no, because if you are alive, you aren't rotting. You'd be quite safe sitting in a bath of maggots. Not happy, but safe.

Here's another surprise. Maggots are used in hospitals. If someone has a wound that won't heal because bacteria have started to kill the flesh, doctors can use maggots to clean it out. They breed the maggots in a very clean lab for this, then put them in the wound and cover it up. Because the maggots only eat *rotting* flesh, they nibble off all the bad bits, and the wound will heal well.

The only problem is the noise. They say that you can hear them chomping away ... Still, I suppose it's worth it.

Chapter 2
Weapons

Sea Slugs

Slugs are boring and dull, right? Wrong.
Just look at the picture. Garden slugs may
be boring, but sea slugs are amazing. Do a
computer search and you'll find dozens, in
all sorts of colours and shapes. They're
armed as well – and they steal their
weapons from another animal.

Sea slugs eat sea creatures that look like shaggy pom-poms, called sea anemones. They have stinging cells at the end of their tentacles to defend themselves. Sadly for the sea anemones, sea slugs don't seem to be bothered by these stings, and they eat anemones whole. A very odd thing happens then. The stings are not broken down in the sea slug's gut. They move through its body and end up at the end of the sea slug's tentacles, where they prevent most things from eating it.

Angler Fish

'Angler' is another word for fisherman. There are lots of different types of angler fish. They have big mouths lined with scary teeth – and they trick smaller fish towards their doom, just like fishermen!

In front of their mouths they dangle something that can look like a worm or a tiny fish. This is called a lure. In fact, it is part of their fin. The angler fish itself is lumpy and patched with colour so that it looks like a rock. It waves the lure around to attract its prey.

Some angler fish live in the deep sea. Very little light gets down that far. Their lures glow in the dark, because they have glowing bacteria in them. The shining lure is hard for small fish to resist. They swim towards the angler fish's mouth to check it out – and are never seen again ...

Electric Eels

Electric eels live in the muddy water of rivers in South America. The muscles on their sides can make electricity, which they use to find their way if the water is too cloudy for them to see where they're going.

They also use electricity to hunt. Some of these eels are a metre and a half long, and can produce quite a large electric current. The electric shock kills their victims. If you ever happen to be near one and plan to pick it up, *don't* – unless you're wearing rubber gloves and rubber boots. If you aren't, the shock will throw you down on the ground.

Boxer Crabs

These are sometimes called 'pom-pom crabs'. It's a good name, because these crabs pull small sea anemones off rocks. They carry them about in their front claws, just like American cheer leaders carry their pom-poms. If anything tries to attack them, the crab just whacks them in the face (if they have one) with a sea anemone. Since the pom-poms have stings, it's a very good defence.

Regal Horned Lizard

This is the animal with my favourite
weapon! The lizard leads a dull life, eating
ants and not doing much else. Unless, that
is, a coyote shows up. Coyotes are wild
dogs from North America. They like to eat
these lizards if they get a chance, but the
lizard has other ideas. If a lizard thinks

it's going to be attacked, it shoots a jet of blood out of its eye socket, often hitting the coyote in the face. This makes the coyote, or any other animal for that matter, think twice before sinking its teeth in. And that gives the lizard time to make an escape.

Japanese Honey Bees

There are honey bees in Japan, and there are honey bees in Europe, and, to you or me, they look much the same. However, only the Japanese ones know how to use the blanket of death.

Japan is home to some seriously large and nasty hornets, which are like very big and very angry wasps. Hornets enjoy chomping their way through hives of honey bees. If they attack bees in Europe, they always win. Just 30 hornets can kill all 30,000 bees in a hive in a few hours (they bite their heads off, in case you were interested). Then they eat the grubs and the honey.

However, if the hornets attack honey bees in Japan, things are different. The honey bees crawl all over the hornets until they form a thick blanket. They don't try to sting, they just cuddle the hornets and vibrate their bodies to raise the heat until it gets up to 47°C. That's OK for the honey bees, but hornets die at 46°C. Hooray for the bees!

Puffer Fish

A puffer fish would make a tasty meal for an otter. Not a good meal, mind you, because it's full of poison, so the otter would end up dead. But the puffer fish would be dead too! From its point of view, it's much better not to be eaten in the first place.

So it's quite easy for an otter to catch a puffer fish, but *much* harder for it to eat it. The puffer fish gulps in air and swells up like a great big ball. The otter suddenly finds it's playing with a big bubble instead of having lunch. After a while, it gets fed up and drops the fish, and the puffer fish lets all the air out and swims off.

Frogs

It's hard to think of a frog as armed and deadly, isn't it? That's because you're not a fly. If a fly wants to stay alive, it needs to keep well away from frogs. A frog that's hunting looks just the same as a frog that's not hunting at all. They both sit still. But a hunting frog is sitting still and waiting for a fly. Frogs' eyes aren't very good at seeing shape or colour, but they are very good at seeing when anything moves. If an insect flies close to a frog, the frog shoots out its tongue, and will often catch it.

A frog's tongue is strong and sticky and very, very long. Inside the frog's mouth it's curled up like one of those party blowers that shoot out at people. The frog's tongue shoots out in the same way (without the stupid noise). Human tongues are attached at the back but frogs' tongues are attached at the front. This lets the tongue shoot out faster, a bit like a whip.

Chapter 3
Weird And Wonderful

Naked Mole Rats

Think of an animal that looks like a very old grey sock with a fork stuck through the toe. That's what naked mole rats look like to me, but some people think they look like a hot dog sausage with a fork sticking out of it! Either way, they're not the best-looking animals in the world.

They have almost no hair, and have very crinkled skin and huge front teeth, but what's really odd about them is the way they live.

They spend all their time under the ground, where they live in really big family groups – anything from 20 to 300 animals. They dig huge networks of tunnels that all join up. They can be many miles long. When they dig they work in teams, one behind the other. The front one uses its huge teeth to dig, and shovels the dirt back with its feet. The others pass the earth back with their feet as well, and the one at the back kicks it above ground and into a heap. Their teeth are *outside* their lips, so their mouths don't fill up with dirt as they dig.

Now, everyone knows that bees, wasps, ants and termites live in a big family group called a colony. But naked mole rats are the only mammals that live like this. Just like bees, they have a 'queen'. She's the only female in the colony who breeds. She chooses a few males to be her mates, and all the other members of the colony do all the work – digging, finding food, looking after the young rats. Some of them are 'soldiers' who defend the colony.

The members of a colony know each other by smell (after all, sight isn't much use under the ground). They keep their smell nice and strong by rolling around in their own pee.

Their tunnels stay fairly warm, and they sleep in a big, hot heap. If they get cold, one of them goes up near the surface where it lies somewhere warm and heats itself up. Then it comes back and acts like a hot water bottle for all the others!

Army Ants

These ants live in South America and Africa. People are very afraid of them. They don't build a proper nest like other ants. They march by day, camp by night, and eat almost anything that gets in their way.

A line or column of army ants can take hours to pass. There can be up to two million ants. Soldiers – blind ants with huge jaws – go near the front and at the sides. Workers carry the young ants right in the middle of the column, where it's safest. Right at the front are the hunters. The hunters swarm over any animal that's too slow to get out of the way, and cut it up with their jaws. They will attack almost anything – scorpions, lizards, birds in nests, as well as smaller things like insects.

Every few weeks they stop for a few days to allow the grubs they've been carrying to turn into adult ants. The queen then lays some more eggs. Quite a lot of eggs in fact – about 300,000. They don't dig a nest, but just hold on to each other so that their bodies form a living nest.

The Sex Life Of Mites

What on earth is a mite? Most people have never seen one, because most of them are only about the size of a full stop. If you've got a pet cat or dog you might have seen them scratch their ears. They do this because some mites live inside their ears and make them itchy.

On the whole they're pretty boring, but some of them have a very strange sex life – even if it's still a boring one.

The female mite makes 15 eggs, which grow inside her body and hatch when they are still inside her body. 14 are always females, and the other one is always male. The male mates with all his sisters, then dies without even having been born! The sisters, who are now pregnant, eat their way out of their mother's body. Then it all starts again. It must be sort of like the bit in the film *Alien* when the alien bursts out of the man's body ...

The Seas Are Alive With The Sound Of ... Herring?

I've never thought much about how fish talk to each other. I don't expect that many people spend a lot of time thinking about this. I might think a bit more about it now that I know what herring do.

Herring talk to each other by farting. Yes, farting! Now, that's a very odd thing to do, but these are clever herring. They can hear the farts (well, it wouldn't really work if they didn't) but the animals that hunt herring can't, because the sound is too high.

Silent but deadly, as they say.

Shrews

A shrew looks like a very small mouse with a pointed nose. Shrews are the smallest mammals. I'm glad, because if they were the size of a dog, they'd be very, very scary!

Shrews are 5.5 to 6 cm long, and weigh between five and 12 grams. Because they are so small, they lose a lot of heat from the surface of their body. Keeping warm takes a lot of energy, and that takes a lot of food. Shrews have to eat every two or three hours or they die. Every day, they eat about 90% of their body weight! That's like a 50 kg human eating 150 pizzas every day!

Shrews eat mainly worms and insects. They have very sharp teeth with red points on them. Some shrews have poison in their spit (saliva) to help them stun really big worms. Their sense of smell is so good that they can sniff out a worm when it's 12 cm under the ground, then dig it out.

Owls often hunt shrews, but don't often eat them, because they taste nasty. Well, if you ate worms you'd taste nasty too.

Sometimes, you can spot young shrews travelling with their mother in what's called a caravan. No, not the sort of caravan you go on holiday in. They all line up behind each other, and each one holds on to the tail of the one in front as they scamper along.

Birds With Itches

Birds like black starlings and jackdaws have a very odd habit. They invite insects like ants to crawl all over them by sitting on ants' nests. Why? Well, the ants eat little insects called parasites that live under birds' feathers. Not surprisingly, the habit is called 'anting'. Some birds will pick up a single ant in their beaks and dab at itchy bits of their skin.

A few birds get so carried away by the feeling that they poke all sorts of odd things at their skin, like wasps, burning leaves, cigarette ends ... All very strange.

Cicadas

Cicadas are bullet-shaped insects with wings. They are found all over the warm parts of the world. They have a very weird life cycle. The males sing loudly from treetops to attract females. After they have mated, the females lay hundreds of eggs in slits in the tree bark. When the young ones hatch, they drop to the ground and dig

down, maybe as much as two metres. They keep alive by sucking the juice from plant roots, and they stay down there for a long, long time. One kind of cicada in the USA stays underground for 17 years! After the 17 years are up, all the cicadas come up to the top. Within a few weeks, they climb up the nearest tree and shed their skins and turn into adults. The males go up to the top of the tree to sing, and the whole life-cycle starts again. All this happens, without fail, every 17 years.

People say that they're good to eat too. How about a chocolate cicada cake, or an apple and cicada pie? I've got the recipes – if you want them!

Green Mice

There are green insects, fish, birds, frogs, lizards – but no green mammals. Sloths are green, but that's only because there are green algae (tiny green plants) in their fur. There is a type of monkey called a Green Monkey, but it's not *very* green.

Scientists in Japan think that there should be green mammals, so they've made some! They took the protein that makes some types of jellyfish green (not just green, in fact, but glow-in-the-dark green) and put it into mouse eggs.

Result? Glowing green mice. Amazing. With two or three of these in your bedroom you could be reading this book by mouse light!

Chapter 4

Lazy Bones

Sloths

Three-toed sloths, to give them their full name, live in South America. They spend almost all their time hanging upside down from trees, and have a very dull life! They eat leaves – only one type of leaf in fact. But that isn't a problem since it's a very common leaf, and no other animals eat it.

Sloths aren't really hunted by anything, but eagles sometimes eat them.

Sloths move very slowly (they have a top speed of about one km per hour) and sleep for about 18 hours a day. They have very weak senses – their hearing is so bad that they hardly notice if a gun is fired near them. They're nearly dumb and can hardly see. I guess they are slow to get bored ...

They make a good home for other living things because they move around so little. They look green because they have green algae living in their fur. There are also moths, whose caterpillars eat any rotten bits of sloth hair.

In fact, there's a job waiting out there for someone. Sloths haven't been studied very much compared with many other animals – they do so little, they're too boring to attract interest!

Termite Queens

Termites look like large, white ants. Every termite colony has a King and Queen, but it's the Queen who wins the prize for being the most lazy. She is stuck inside the middle of the colony, and is too fat to fit down any of the narrow tunnels to get out.

She is fed, groomed and waited on by the colony's workers. She is much, much bigger than the workers. Her abdomen (the lower part of her body) can be 12 cm long. It needs to be, since her job is to lay eggs. Lots of eggs. 30,000 a day, in fact. So she needs a big abdomen to keep them in. Come to think of it, maybe she isn't so lazy after all.

Lions

Lions are great, powerful hunters who rule the African plains ... Well, no.

Lions are lazy lumps, bullying other animals to give up what they have caught, lying asleep on the African plains for hours and hours ... Yes, that's right.

There are two ways that lions like to spend their time. Their second one is eating, but it's sleeping that comes way out in front. If you own a pet cat, you'll know that cats in general are very keen on sleeping, but the lion is the champion. An adult lion will sleep for 20 hours every day if it gets the chance. That's more than a sloth!

Everyone's seen films of lions hunting some poor animal like a zebra, and they are very good at it. However, if they find a leopard or cheetah with something it's killed, they take it away from them. Lions can do this because they are heavier and stronger than the other animal. If it tried to fight back it would get hurt or killed. The poor leopard or cheetah has to slink off and start all over again. Lions aren't so great after all – they're lazy bullies. So there.

Tardigrades

Come on now, you've never heard of these, have you? Tardigrades. Not easy to say or see. And yet, they're all around you. Their other names are "water bear" and, even better, "moss piglet". They are tiny (0.3 to 1 mm) creatures that live in clumps of green moss.

Tardigrades are fat and slow and cuddly looking, and have eight pairs of legs with claws at the ends. They move about slowly, doing not very much, but they are very,

very good at staying alive in very difficult conditions. They do this by going into a kind of deep sleep called hibernation. They can keep on sleeping even when it's minus 200°C (very, very cold) or when it's 150°C (very, very hot).

It takes 1,000 times as much nuclear radiation to kill a tardigrade as it does to kill a human. If tardigrades are dried out you can add water and they come back to life. Some have been brought back to life in this way after being dried out in a bit of moss for 120 years!

I think they'd make great pets if they were a bit bigger. After all, you wouldn't have to worry about them if you went away on holiday. Just let them dry out when you go, and add water when you come home again!

Chapter 5
Fantastic Facts
Big

Giant squid are hardly ever seen, as they live deep in the sea. One was washed up on a beach in New Zealand in 1933. It was 21 metres long, with 40 cm wide eyes.

The **robber crab** lives on land, only going back to the sea to breed. It climbs coconut trees and cuts down coconuts to eat. Its legs are a metre long, so they can stretch all the way round the tree trunk.

The **goliath bird-eating spider** has a leg span a scary 28 cm wide. Eek! That means its legs stretch further than the edges of this open book. Maybe if you had a really well trained pet one, you could get it to hold the book up for you.

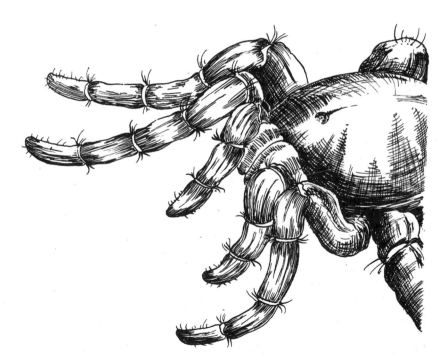

The insect that weighs the most is the **goliath beetle**. It can weigh up to 100 grams. That's the same as an apple.

The **giant catfish** is the largest fresh-water fish in the world. It is only found at the mouth of a river called the Mekong in Vietnam. It can grow over three metres long and can weigh almost 300 kg. You'd need a lot of chips to go with that.

An **ostrich**, the tallest bird in the world, can lay eggs that weigh up to 2.35 kg. The eggs are very strong. You can stand on one and it won't break.

German giant rabbits can be a metre long from head to little fluffy tail, and can weigh over 10 kg.

Small

A bird in Jamaica, called the **vervain humming bird**, lays eggs less than 10 mm long. That's smaller than a baked bean! How on earth does a bird – even a tiny one – fit in that space?

The shortest fish in the world is another kind of **angler fish**. This one is only 6.2 mm long. What I want to know is, how did they find it?

The smallest bird is the **bee humming bird**. It's less than 6 cm long and weighs 1.6 grams. (That's only half of what a 5p piece weighs.)

Opossums are small mammals that live in North America. Their babies are so tiny that you can fit 15 of them on a tablespoon when they're born (but I can't imagine why you would want to).

Poisonous

Jack jumper ants from Tasmania in Australia have a sting so powerful it can kill people who are sensitive to it.

One **golden poison dart frog** contains enough poison to kill 1,500 people. But why would it want to? It's not some sort of James Bond villain with a plan to take over the world. Or is it?

The most deadly of all snakes is the **coastal taipan**. One bite has enough poison to kill 120 people. That must be an example of over-kill (ha ha).

It's not the most poisonous, but I think the most scary snake is the **black mamba**. It can move very fast indeed. Some people say it can go up to 23 km per hour. Do you think you could run faster than that?

Some of the most poisonous fish in the world are **puffer fish**. (These aren't the same ones the otters try to juggle.) If you ever write a crime novel, it's worth knowing about them, because their poison cannot be detected. Just right for the perfect murder! You wouldn't think anyone would want to eat them, would you? But they're very popular in Japan. The chef has to be good at preparing it, though. If he doesn't take out all the bits he should, your tongue goes numb. And then you die.

Just Plain Strange

The **tapir**, a pig-like animal with a long nose, is the only animal with 14 toes.

12....13....14

May-flies are insects that only live for one day. **Giant tortoises** live for over 100 years.

Fleas can jump 20 times their own body length. That's like a person jumping over 30 metres.

In winter when **hamsters** hibernate, their heart only beats six times every minute. It's very hard to tell a dead hamster from one that is sleeping.

There are lizards called **chameleons** that can shoot out their tongues at over 20 km per hour.

The **wood frog** can survive being frozen solid for weeks without dying.

The **Arctic tern** is a bird that flies from the Arctic to the Antarctic and back again every year. That's about 35,000 km.

The loneliest animal in the world may well be Lonesome George. He is the only **Abingdon Island giant tortoise** still alive. Awww ...

Armadillos can hold their breath for up to six minutes. This has led people to believe that when they come to rivers they just hold their breath and walk across the bottom.

Frozen animals really do fall from the sky sometimes! There are records of small turtles, squid, geese and ducks crashing down, and at least one story of a frozen squirrel breaking a car windscreen.

Honeypot ants force feed some of their workers with nectar (sweet juice from flowers) until their bodies swell to the size of a pea. Then they hang them up by their front legs on the walls of the nest to act as living honey jars.

Barrington Stoke would like to thank all its readers for commenting on the manuscript before publication and in particular:

Jessica Armstrong
Val Boycott
Debbie Campbell
Jennifer Collins
Danny Duffy
Laura Evans
Lisa-Jane Fieldsend
Charlotte Hanson
Agnes MacKenzie
Kimberley Ritchie
Tasha Sime
Mark Small
Shannon Stockdale
Julie Sutherland
Sherin Thomas
Charlotte White

Become a Consultant!

Would you like to give us feedback on our titles before they are published? Contact us at the e-mail address below – we'd love to hear from you!

info@barringtonstoke.co.uk
www.barringtonstoke.co.uk

AUTHOR CHECK LIST

Gill Arbuthnott

Do you have any pets? What are they called?

I have a big bad cat called Len. Before that I had a cat called Bodger who was deaf and only had one eye. He was a real softy, but I have to be careful with Len, or I lose fingers!

What animal are you most scared of?

My children? No, wait – dogs who wear bandannas around their necks. They're always called something like 'Tyson', and they look like steaks with teeth.

What's the oddest thing you've ever eaten?

The strangest thing would have to be lamb intestine soup. It's something that the Greeks eat for Easter. It tasted mostly of pepper ...

Which would you rather find in your bedroom: a Goliath Bird-Eating Spider or a Golden Poison Dart Frog?

I didn't even have to think about that one. Give me the frog any time. Even the drawing of the spider in the book creeps me out. Too many legs.

ILLUSTRATOR CHECK LIST

Shona Grant

Do you have any pets? What are they called?

I've got lots of pets. A dog called Ruby, a cat called Minty, two guinea pigs called Scribble and Chalky (my daughters' pets) and a terrapin I've had for 22 years, called Terrence (although it's a girl).

What animal are you most scared of?

Spiders. They're really creepy.

What's the oddest thing you've ever eaten?

When I was little I ate chocolate-coated ants. Yum!

What's the craziest thing you've ever done?

Not too crazy, but revolting. I found a sheep's skull on the beach and took it back to the flat that I was staying in. I wanted to draw it. When I woke up the next morning there were loads of maggots pouring out of it. I cunningly thought putting it in a bath full of water would kill the maggots. It did, but someone went into the bathroom to have a bath before I could clean up the mess. Ooops!

Try another book in the
REALITY CHECK
series

Dick Turpin: Legends and Lies
by Terry Deary

Escape From Colditz
by Deborah Chancellor

The Last Duel
by Martyn Beardsley

All available from our website:
www.barringtonstoke.co.uk

Coming soon ...

Pocket Hero
by Pippa Goodhart

The amazing true story of Jeffrey Hudson.
Jeffrey was a human pet, a slave, a Captain
in the army, killed a man in a duel, and was
captured by pirates. And he was only
45 cm tall!

The Land Of Whizzing Arrows
by Simon Chapman

Terrifying true story of explorer Leo
Parcus. Jungles and jaguars, crocodiles and
cannibals. Watch out – this book bites!

All available from our website:
www.barringtonstoke.co.uk